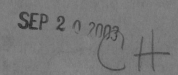

Bethany Roberts

Rosie to the Rescue

illustrated by Kay Chorao

Henry Holt and Company • New York

Henry Holt and Company, LLC
Publishers since 1866
115 West 18th Street
New York, New York 10011
www.henryholt.com

Library of Congress Cataloging-in-Publication Data
Roberts, Bethany.
Rosie to the rescue / by Bethany Roberts; illustrated by Kay Chorao.
Summary: As she waits with her Aunt Lily for her parents, Rosie imagines
all sorts of dangers that might befall them and how she will save them.
[1. Squirrels—Fiction. 2. Imagination—Fiction. 3. Parent and child—Fiction.
4. Aunts—Fiction.] I. Chorao, Kay, ill. II. Title.
PZ7.R5396 Ro 2003   2002004008
ISBN 0-8050-6486-9 / First Edition—2003
Designed by Martha Rago
Printed in the United States of America on acid-free paper. ∞
1 3 5 7 9 10 8 6 4 2

The artist used gouache, colored pencil, and pen and ink to create the illustrations for this book.

"But a dreadful sea serpent
might rise up from the deep."
    "Oh, dear, not that!" said Aunt Lily,
chewing her nails.

"But I would shout at him
and tell his mother,
and he would let them go,"
said Rosie.
    "Aren't you brave!"
said Aunt Lily.

"But a tidal wave might sweep them to
a hungry fox's den."

"Goodness gracious! Perish the thought!"
said Aunt Lily.

"I would tell jokes," said Rosie,
"and make that fox laugh so hard,
he wouldn't see them slip away."
   "You do tell good jokes," said Aunt Lily.

"But an avalanche of boulders
might start to fall on them."
"This gets worse and worse,"
said Aunt Lily, wringing her tail.

"But I would throw those rocks
back up the mountain," said Rosie,
"and they would be safe."
"My, you are strong," said Aunt Lily.

"But a mermaid might sing enchanting songs and make them stay with her forever."

"Forever? That would be terrible!" said Aunt Lily.

"But I would sing songs, too,
and tell them how much I love them,"
said Rosie. "And they would come
right home to me."

"Of course they would," said Aunt Lily.

"And here they are . . .

. . . right on time."